D1068075

BY ALI BOVIS   ILLUSTRATED BY JEN TAYLOR

SYLVIE
Organizer Extraordinaire

WINTER coat DRIVE!

DONATE COATS HERE!

FOR MOM, DAD, BECCA, SUE, STEVE, JENELL, AND
JIM, FOR ALL YOUR ENCOURAGEMENT AND LOVE. —AB

FOR MARC AND MY FAMILY —JT

abdobooks.com

Published by Magic Wagon, a division of ABDO, PO Box 398166,
Minneapolis, Minnesota 55439. Copyright © 2020 by Abdo Consulting
Group, Inc. International copyrights reserved in all countries. No part
of this book may be reproduced in any form without written permission
from the publisher. Calico™ is a trademark and logo of Magic Wagon.

Printed in the United States of America, North Mankato, Minnesota.
102019
012020

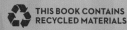

Written by Ali Bovis
Illustrated by Jen Taylor
Edited by Bridget O'Brien
Art Directed by Candice Keimig

Library of Congress Control Number: 2019942288

Publisher's Cataloging-in-Publication Data

Names: Bovis, Ali, author. | Taylor, Jen, illustrator.
Title: Organizer extraordinaire / by Ali Bovis ; illustrated by Jen Taylor.
Description: Minneapolis, Minnesota : Magic Wagon, 2020. | Series: Sylvie; book 3
Summary: Sylvie wants to win her school's talent show so she can be featured in the local
    newspaper to create buzz for her coat drive, but she struggles to figure out her talent.
Identifiers: ISBN 9781532136535 (lib. bdg.) | ISBN 9781644943212 (pbk.) | ISBN 9781532137136
    (ebook) | ISBN 9781532137433 (Read-to-Me ebook)
Subjects: LCSH: Talent shows--Juvenile fiction. | Newspapers--Local editions--Juvenile fiction.
    | Collection boxes (Fund raising equipment)--Juvenile fiction. | Coats--Juvenile fiction. |
    Talents-Juvenile fiction. | Self-assurance--Juvenile fiction. | Friendship--Juvenile fiction
Classification: DDC [Fic]--dc23

TABLE OF CONTENTS

COATS & YELLOW JACKETS

Sylvie rolled up her sleeves. She took a big gulp from her water bottle and fanned herself with a flyer. She peered inside the donation box and examined the contents.

One newspaper. One bee costume. And an old milk carton. She shook her head and whispered, "Seriously?"

Sylvie's teacher, Ms. Martin, popped into the hallway. "Ready?"

Sylvie straightened the "Winter Coat Drive!" poster on her easel. She tightened her hair ribbon and turned up the volume on her megaphone. "Ready!"

The school secretary, Ms. Thompson, hurried down the corridor. She pressed a button on her walkie-talkie. "Bus one, bus two, bus three, check," she said. She balanced supplies for the nurse's office and a stack of lunch calendars. "Morning, Sylvie!"

"Thanks for the donation box, Ms. Thompson," Sylvie replied.

Ms. Thompson gave her a thumbs-up and pushed open the double doors.

The bell rang. Kids poured into the building and filled the halls, heading toward their classrooms.

Sylvie's megaphone screeched. "Good morning, Sea View Elementary! I've got a most important announcement!" she yelled.

A few kids stopped. Most kept walking. Someone tossed a banana peel into Sylvie's donation box.

Well I never! Sylvie thought. "Really?" she exclaimed into the megaphone.

It had been a whole week since the winter coat drive started. But she was getting nowhere.

It didn't help that it had been so hot lately. Coats and jackets must be the last thing on anyone's mind.

All around her, kids were dressed in T-shirts and shorts. Usually by November, it was a cool seventy-five degrees in Sylvie's California seaside town. Ninety degrees was hardly ideal to get into the winter coat drive spirit!

Sylvie's best friend, Sammy, was the first to stop by. He tugged the zipper of his overstuffed backpack and yanked out three puffer coats.

A huge smile spread across Sylvie's face. That was more like it.

She went on, louder. "As I was saying, I have an important announcement. You may recall, my winter coat drive kicked off last week. I'm collecting coats for people in need.

"For people in Sea View and also for New York City, where my grandparents, aunt, uncle, and cousin live. Because it can get especially cold there, and lots of other places as well. And many people don't have coats to keep them warm. It's going to be the biggest and most stellar coat drive ever!"

Sylvie's former best friend, Camilla, walked over. The puffball charm on her backpack bounced up and down. She peeked into the box, raised an eyebrow, and giggled.

"I knew you were collecting coats and jackets. But yellow jackets too?"

Sylvie shook her head. Of course Camilla would have seen the yellow jacket bee costume. And of course she would make a joke about it.

Someone must've taken the "coat or jacket" line in her flyer too literally. But still, it could keep someone warm. And the wings had been bedazzled beautifully. Sylvie smiled. "I really do welcome all coats or jackets."

Just then, Sylvie noticed her friend Josh about to throw a juice box in a trash bin.

His twin brother, Nick, elbowed him. He pointed to the donation box. "You heard Sylvie. Recycle."

Sylvie's eyes widened. It was nice of Nick to think about recycling. Especially after her recycling-themed Halloween party last month.

But she had not been talking about recycling here. Nick was still missing the point. They all were. Were they even listening to her?

"This is not a recycle bin for newspapers, juice boxes, or milk cartons. It is not a food compost bin for banana peels. It's also not a collection site for Halloween costumes, no matter how pretty and sparkly they are. It's for coat donations, to keep people warm this winter."

"Oh!" said Nick.

Josh nodded. "Awesome!"

Sylvie smiled. They were getting it! "Not everyone has enough money for coats. Some people need help staying warm in the winter."

Sylvie noticed a few kids starting to nod and smile. "It may feel hot now, but it will be colder soon. Especially in New

York," she said into the megaphone. "Please bring me your coats. Your long coats. Short coats. Fuzzy coats. Reversible coats. And coats that have secret inside pockets."

"I'll bring one tomorrow," promised Malik. "It's too small for me now, but it will fit someone."

"Me too," said Tori. "My old coat has three layers. My dad calls them the 'California layer,' the 'Chicago layer,' and the 'Christmas at the North Pole' layer. I only wore the California layer. Maybe someone else can use them all!"

"My mom used to live in Maine," said Lori. "It can get cold there. She has tons."

Sylvie rocked on her feet. "Stellar!"

She was on her way! It was a good thing, especially since she had told the charity organization to expect the biggest coat donation in history.

Suddenly, Sylvie's palms started to feel sweaty. And it wasn't from the heat wave. "Alright people, now spread the word. Please! We need all the coats we can get."

MEATBALL MADNESS MONDAYS

The morning bell rang. Sylvie packed up her megaphone and flyers, and she hurried into Ms. Martin's classroom.

She didn't mean to knock Camilla's water bottle off her desk. Or her puffball water bottle cozy either. She scooped them up quickly. "Sorry!"

Camilla made a face. Then she turned to Sylvie and whispered, "Buzz . . ."

Buzz? thought Sylvie.

Would Camilla forget about the bee costume already? Then Sylvie realized, of course. That was it! That was how she could collect the most coats and keep people warm.

Camilla hadn't meant to help. But she had given Sylvie the most stellar idea.

Sylvie tapped Camilla. "Buzzzzzzz!"

Camilla laughed. Then she made a confused face. "Wait, what?" she asked.

Sylvie just smiled.

As Ms. Martin wrote on the board, Sylvie opened her notebook and started to hum her favorite tune. Thanks to her former friend (and that bee costume), Sylvie had figured out the key to making her coat drive a success.

Buzz. As in getting the word out. Sylvie needed to create more buzz and spread the word. The more people who knew about the coat drive, the more coats she could collect.

The more coats she could collect, the more people who would be kept warm this winter. And the more Sylvie would be responsible for the biggest coat drive in history. Not, of course, that that last one mattered. Much.

But creating buzz could take time. She would need to get started right away. Her hand shot up.

Ms. Martin was writing a list of spelling words.

Sylvie waved both arms. Nothing. She'd have to wait until her teacher was finished at the board.

Sylvie flipped through her planner and gasped. She tipped her chair forward and nudged Sammy.

Sammy swung around. Sylvie held up five fingers. "Only five days left for the coat drive," she whispered.

Sammy straightened his glasses. "Five days?" he whispered back. "Yikes."

Yikes was right. She needed to hurry.

Sylvie tapped her pencil. She cleared her throat. She couldn't wait any longer. "Ms. Martin?" she blurted. "Ms. Martin!"

Ms. Martin turned. "Yes? Do you have a question, Sylvie?"

But as Sylvie was about to answer, Principal Close's voice blared over the speaker.

No! Not morning announcements. They could go on forever. Especially on a Monday!

Ms. Martin held up her hand. "Hold that thought," she said softly.

Sylvie sighed. She would have to wait. Again.

She started to copy the spelling words as Principal Close went on. Then she turned a page in her notebook and started a list of how to create buzz.

Sylvie heard bits of what the principal was saying. But mostly, she was plotting her buzz-building plan.

When Principal Close wrapped up with her joke of the day, Ms. Martin pointed to Sylvie.

Sylvie stood at her desk. "I need to create buzz for my coat drive," she said. "If I read my list, can everyone help me spread the word?"

Sylvie didn't wait for a response. She read her list.

How to Create Buzz for the Coat Drive:

Post more flyers around town

Go door to door

Hold a phone and texting party

Email the neighborhood, friends, family

Partner with businesses and other schools

But her classmates didn't appear to be completely focused.

Even worse, Sylvie had a feeling that there was something especially interesting and important Principal Close had said during announcements. The only problem was Sylvie couldn't remember what.

Had Principal Close said something important?

There had been something right between the cafeteria's announcement of Meatball Madness Monday and the math club meeting time change.

But what?

CREATING BUZZ

It was a long morning of creative writing and times tables.

The recess bell rang. *Finally*, thought Sylvie. She raced to the door. All the schoolwork and worrying about buzz had been exhausting. Thankfully it was nothing a good game of freeze tag couldn't cure.

Outside, Sylvie dashed across the playground to base. "Safe!" she called.

No one was there. *That's strange,* thought Sylvie.

She looked around. No one was playing tag. Not only that—no one was on the swings, the monkey bars, or the hopscotch boards. Even the four square courts were empty! *What in the world?*

Sammy came over.

"Hey," said Sylvie. "Do you know where everyone went?"

Sammy pointed to the grass. "Up there."

"I wonder what they're doing." Sylvie walked with Sammy to the playground.

She spotted Camilla cartwheeling. Tori and Lori were practicing pliés and arabesques. Malik, Josh, and Nick were making funny faces.

Who knows what that's about, thought Sylvie.

Sammy was kneeling. Something squeaked below him. He recorded a note in his reptile observations journal. "Want to look for lizards?"

Sylvie loved examining reptiles with Sammy. Last week they found a rare blue-tailed skink. Helping Sammy would be just as fun as freeze tag! She crouched down and sifted through the grass.

"Sure," she said, crawling. "But after, can we brainstorm more ideas for creating buzz for the coat drive? I know I'm missing something. Something else that can really get it going."

Sammy nodded. Something green scampered right underneath their noses. Sammy jotted a note. Sylvie giggled and kept crawling.

Sammy took off after the creature as Camilla cartwheeled over. "Are you practicing crawling for the talent show?"

Sylvie looked up. Crawling? She was doing important observation work to protect the future of reptiles from extinction. Anyway, what was Camilla talking about? "What talent show?"

"What talent show?" Camilla spun the honor roll bracelet on her wrist.

"Only the biggest talent show in the history of Sea View Elementary. It's this Friday. Tons of kids have acts. Even some teachers."

The talent show! That must have been what Principal Close had been talking about during announcements.

Maybe it was what all those announcements the past few weeks had been about, too. Hard to say. Sylvie's favorite time to dream up plans and make lists to save the world was during morning announcements.

That was why no one was playing tag

or anything else. The talent show was just days away. They were practicing their acts.

"That's cool," said Sylvie. Her friends did have amazing talents. It would be fun to see the show and cheer them on. Then she realized the timing. "But my coat drive ends Friday too, so I'll probably be too busy to go."

Camilla tightened her bracelet. "You don't need to go anyway. You can read about it in the newspaper."

Sylvie did a double take. "In the newspaper?"

"That's right." Camilla puffed out her chest. "The winning act will be featured in the *Sea View Times*."

Wow! Sylvie had always wanted to be in the *Sea View Times*.

Just then Sammy sprinted toward them. He swatted his hand back and forth. "Bees!" He kept running.

Sylvie and Camilla scattered.

As Sylvie ran, her eyes opened wide. Bees! She had just figured out how to create the biggest buzz of all. She yelled to Sammy. "Be careful! Meet you at the swings!"

Before long, Camilla was back to cartwheeling. Sylvie and Sammy hopped on their swings and pumped their legs high above the playground.

During his upswing, Sammy straightened his glasses with one hand. "That was close."

"You know you're not supposed to swat them," said Sylvie. "You told me yourself! Plus, some types of bees are even endangered. Be careful next time, for their sake. But anyway, their timing was perfect!"

"Yeah," said Sammy. "Wait, huh?"

"The bees," said Sylvie. "The bees and their buzz. I know how to get the most buzz.

"If I win the talent show, I'll be in the paper. I can announce the coat drive. I'll extend the deadline, and then everyone will know about it and donate coats. Then it really will be the biggest coat drive ever. Just imagine all the people we can help keep warm."

"That's a great idea," said Sammy. "I didn't even know you had a talent."

Sylvie pumped her legs and leaned back as far as she could. "Neither did I!"

SKYDIVING AND OTHER TALENTS

Sylvie dropped by the front office at dismissal time and found the talent show sign-up sheet on the wall.

Ms. Thompson was filing permission slips for a class trip. "How's the coat drive going?" she asked.

Sylvie shuffled from one foot to another. "Not so great."

"I'm sorry to hear that," said Ms. Thompson. "I loved your flyers around school. The hallway, the cafeteria, and I think I even found a few in the bathroom."

Sylvie perked up. "Thanks. I tried to cover the key spots. But I need to get my message out beyond school. And now I know how to do it."

"Need any help?" asked Ms. Thompson.

"Do you have a pen? I want to write my name on the talent show sign-up sheet," said Sylvie. "I have to win so I can spread the word about the coat drive in the newspaper."

Ms. Thompson placed the permission slips in a cabinet. "That's a wonderful idea." She handed Sylvie a pen. "Good luck!"

Sylvie examined the sign-up sheet. Camilla had written her act on the first line: "Camilla Garcia: Gymnast Extraordinaire."

Camilla had taken tumbling classes since they were in preschool. She was a gymnast extraordinaire. She probably had something stellar planned.

Sylvie took in the list of acts. "Wow," she whispered.

After Camilla, everyone else had called themselves "extraordinaires" too. "Dancer Extraordinaire," "Karate Chopper Extraordinaire," "Hot Dog Eater Extraordinaire." All that talent, in her very own class! Who knew?

Sylvie looked up and noticed Sammy's "Reptiles Rule" hat bobbing past the "Choose Kindness" mural in the hallway. "Thanks, Ms. Thompson!"

She scribbled her name on the last line. She'd have to figure out her act later, she realized, racing off.

"Sammy!" Sylvie called, running outside.

Her best friend looked up from his book, *How to Train Your Bearded Dragon*.

"Want to come over and help me plan my act?" asked Sylvie. "Want to help me win the talent show?"

Sammy swung his backpack around and shoved his book inside. "Sure. What are you going to do?"

Sylvie whipped out paper and a pencil. "Now *that* is the question!"

Before the safety patrol monitor could close Sylvie's car door, she and Sammy had already come up with three exciting ideas. Skydiving, knife throwing, and fire eating.

At home, they raced inside.

"Don't forget, you and Henry need to walk Snickers," said her dad.

"Got it!" Sylvie said.

She grabbed her puppy, Snickers, and a handful of cookies. "Henry!"

Her little brother ambled downstairs, his nose stuck in a bag of chips.

"Henry, hurry!" Sylvie said.

As Sylvie, Henry, Sammy, and Snickers walked, Sylvie started to worry. "I'm not sure those acts are right for me," she confided to Sammy.

She wasn't exactly trained in skydiving, not to mention knife throwing or fire eating. "I might need something different."

Henry popped a cookie into his

mouth. "What about eating a ton of snickerdoodles?"

It would definitely be the most delicious act, Sylvie thought. She tightened the leash to keep Snickers from the road.

But everyone knew Zaki could eat the most hot dogs in Sea View. He probably had eating massive amounts of food covered. "Thanks. Maybe something not involving eating."

Sammy pointed to Sylvie's puppy, trotting next to her, his ears flapping. "What about training Snickers? You could create a whole act."

Just then, Snickers barked at a squirrel as if it were a fifty-foot bear. He dragged Sylvie after it and wiped out on a tree root by Josh and Nick's house.

Sylvie helped the dog up. "Maybe you're not *quite* ready for the stage."

Sounds floated out from Josh and Nick's garage. Josh, Nick, and Malik were singing. Then Camilla tumbled down the driveway in a hot pink leotard. They must have gotten together to practice for the talent show.

"Whoa!" Camilla yelled, landing. "Achoo, achoo, achoo!"

Henry and Sammy caught up.

"Wow. Camilla's pretty good. Even with all that sneezing," said Sammy. "Josh, Nick, and Malik, too."

Sylvie stood there watching Camilla turn cartwheels in the driveway and listening to the boys' singing. Sammy was right.

The singing was spectacular. The tumbles were tremendous. Extraordinary even. Either one of their acts would win the talent show. Either one of them would be featured in the newspaper.

Sylvie felt a jolt. Two jolts, actually. One on her arm as Snickers tugged his leash toward the house.

And one in Sylvie's head as a big realization hit her. If she wanted to win the talent show and spread the word about the coat drive, there was only one thing she could do.

Well, two things, actually.

GYMNAST EXTRAORDINAIRE

Over the years, Sylvie had done both gymnastics and singing. Her friends were not the only ones who could be extraordinaires. Probably. She needed to revive one of her old talents—or both of them, for good measure.

Camilla was sitting on the driveway digging a pebble out of her ear.

Sylvie ran up to her. "Stellar floor routine!" she shouted.

Camilla pulled twigs from her hair. She picked mulch off her leotard and refastened the torn brown Band-Aids dangling off her elbow. "Yes, well, I did that on purpose."

Sylvie smiled. "Awesome back handsprings!" It did look like a great finale. Even if those bruises hurt. "You have a great act. I was thinking it might be even better if I joined in too. Can I perform with you?"

Camilla covered her hands in powdered chalk. She walked along a crack in the cement, practicing her balance beam routine. From the look of her narrowed eyes, Sylvie guessed Camilla was suspicious of her offer.

"You're entering the talent show?" Camilla asked. "I don't know. What about your coat drive? Will you have time to do both?"

"I'm going to perform in the talent show to create the biggest buzz of all," explained Sylvie. She nudged Snickers off Camilla's cement crack.

"You can't get bigger than an announcement in the *Sea View Times*. And I can tell everyone about my coat drive. Then I can collect more coats than ever."

Camilla lifted onto her toes and twirled. "The *Sea View Times* is a big deal."

Sylvie held her breath. Was Camilla really going to agree to Sylvie performing with her?

Camilla pinched up her face and shook her head. "But you don't have any gymnastics experience." She arched an eyebrow. "Do you?"

Sylvie smiled as she remembered the gold ribbon pinned to her bulletin board. She nodded. "I do! I even won an award!"

Surely her Tumble Tuesdays teacher thought Sylvie was a gymnast extraordinaire. Her gold ribbon had "Participation" printed on it and everything. Not anyone could earn that, Sylvie figured.

Camilla narrowed her eyes again. "An award, huh? I had no idea you were such a talented gymnast. I guess you can join my act."

Camilla showed Sylvie her act. The forward rolls! The backward cartwheels!

The double flips! For the finale, she landed with her feet together, arms raised triumphantly.

"Well," Camilla said. "Ready to try?"

Sylvie rubbed her hands and forced a smile. "Um," was all she got out.

A wave of dizziness spread over Sylvie, and she hadn't even been the

one spinning. Sylvie realized that some of these moves might not have been covered at Tumble Tuesdays.

Camilla's face showed panic. "What? Did I do something wrong? Could the act be better?"

That gave Sylvie an idea. The act could be better. If Sylvie wanted to perform with Camilla and win together, it would need to be.

"I think it could," Sylvie replied.

She felt the ideas bubbling up inside her. Like swapping out those old brown Band-Aids, for starters.

Sylvie called to Sammy and Henry, who were talking to Josh and Nick's mom, Ms. Johnston. "Can you take Snickers home?" she asked.

Henry petted behind the dog's ears. "Sure," said Sammy, taking Snickers's leash.

Sylvie pulled out her planner. She made notes about Camilla's act until there was no white left on the paper and no chalk left in the driveway.

"Hello?" said Camilla.

Sylvie looked up to find Camilla waving her hands in Sylvie's face.

"If you're going to perform with me, you need to learn the act," said Camilla.

"I know," said Sylvie. "I just need to organize a few more things."

"Organize?" asked Camilla.

"I'll explain later," said Sylvie, heading toward the house. "I need to work on the laser lights."

"Laser lights? For what?" asked Camilla.

Sylvie giggled. "For our grand finale, of course."

GO ON WITH A BANG!

It had taken a quick search on Ms. Johnston's computer to find a company specializing in laser lights. But they were all set now.

Sylvie ran out of the Johnstons' kitchen. She interrupted Camilla mid-back handspring. "I just had the most amazing call with the laser-light people," she said.

Camilla made a funny face. "What's

that?" She pointed to the binder in Sylvie's arms.

It was lucky that Ms. Johnston had a spare binder. How else could Sylvie have presented Camilla with the notes, plans, and laser-light show details she had printed out? "I started organizing everything. Look."

Camilla flipped through the binder. "What's this?"

"I have renamed the act," Sylvie said. "Gymnasts Extraordinaire was all right, but—"

"But what?" Camilla asked.

"If we are going to be in the *Sea View Times*, and if we really want to create buzz for the coat drive, we need something catchier."

Camilla put her hand on her waist. "Like what?"

Sylvie stood tall as she smiled. "Gymnasts Extraordinaire for Good!" she pronounced.

Camilla nodded. "Huh. I like it! But it's time for my piano lesson. I've got to go."

Sylvie checked her Save the Rain Forest watch. The hour hand was in the monkey habitat. Yikes, it had gotten late! She had spent her time planning and no time practicing.

She still had a gymnastics routine to learn. Not to mention Sylvie had not yet shared the good news with Josh, Nick, and Malik that she'd be joining *their* act for the talent show too!

Sylvie hurried into the garage. The boys were harmonizing. They hit all the high notes, and their pitch was perfect. Sylvie took it in. She shimmied her shoulders and tapped her feet.

"Stellar performance!" she cheered.

And it really was. Josh, Nick, and Malik's act might have been even better than Camilla's. Yep, Sylvie would definitely need to join their act, too.

They didn't need as many new Band-Aids as Camilla. Still, the act could use some pop. Some pizzazz. With a little planning and some fireworks, Sylvie, Josh, Nick, and Malik could croon their way to the cover of the *Sea View Times*.

As the boys sang, Sylvie turned a page. She started a new list:

Music Act

1. Costumes

2. *Choreography*

3. *Indoor environmentally-friendly nonflammable-fireworks show?*

"Fireworks would really make the act go on with a bang!" said Sylvie.

She shared her other ideas. The boys immediately agreed that Sylvie would help organize their act and perform with them, too.

"Anything for fireworks," Nick had said.

Soon, the sun faded. A breeze blew up the block. The cold weather was coming.

A grin came across Sylvie's face. By the weekend, she would have both acts down pat. One of the acts had to win.

She could imagine the *Sea View Times* already. People would be sending in coats from everywhere. Every cold person would be warm.

Sylvie hugged her binder. With a bit more organizing and some practice, she'd be set. Now she needed to get a good fireworks team on board.

THE COLD
IS COMING

Sylvie's grandparents called that night to report that a snowstorm was barreling toward New York. "Awesome!" Sylvie had said when she first heard the news.

Sylvie's mom told her how much fun snowstorms had been when she was a kid. They meant no school, snowball fights, and lots of hot cocoa with extra marshmallows.

Sylvie didn't know a lot about snowstorms. But they sure sounded like fun. Sylvie bet Snickers would love them. Henry, too.

She tried to imagine a snow day in Sea View. Would people make snow angels in the sand? Sip hot cocoa on the cactus farm? Ski on the beach dunes?

"Time for bed," Sylvie's mom yelled from the kitchen.

"Ready in a minute," Sylvie said.

She threw on her pajamas and brushed her teeth, then snuck into the den and turned on the national news.

New York City was already dusted in a thin layer of the white powder.

"Stellar!" Sylvie whispered.

A reporter came into the frame. "It's likely to be a cold morning, with temperatures dipping well below freezing," he said. "Everyone needs to bundle up tomorrow!"

Suddenly she got a sinking feeling. She shouldn't be thinking about hot cocoa. She should be thinking about the people who needed warm winter coats. And winning the talent show to advertise her coat drive.

Sylvie hurried to her room and tucked herself into bed. She had a busy day ahead of her.

The next morning, Sylvie woke early, fed Snickers, and flipped on the weather channel. By now, the snow would be covering everything.

Sylvie bet it would be packed as high as the Empire State Building. So many people would be needing her coats!

But when she found a report from New York, something funny came across the screen: a mother duck and her ducklings paddling across a sun-drenched pond. A turtle catching rays on a rock. Joggers zipped past the news camera wearing *shorts?*

There was no snow. No ice. It didn't even look cold! Huh?

Sylvie flipped through the channels, thinking she had the wrong one. Wasn't it supposed to be the storm of the century?

"Sylvie!" called her dad. "Time for school!"

A little later, as Sylvie unpacked her bag at school, she thought about the weatherman's explanation. Apparently the storm had stayed out at sea.

At first, Sylvie had felt disappointed. But when she thought about it, she realized it was a lucky break. Now she had more time to gather coats and get them to the people who needed them most. Because another storm would come, any day!

Sylvie hurried to the bulletin board, tripping on a bag along the way.

Ms. Martin looked up from her desk. "Good morning. Is everything OK, Sylvie?"

Sylvie picked up her flyers and raced to her teacher. "Ms. Martin, a big snowstorm was expected in New York. Thank goodness the weather reports were wrong. But still, it's going to get colder every day."

Ms. Martin flicked on her desktop fan. She fidgeted with the controls and pushed the setting to high. "I hope so!"

Sylvie fanned herself with the flyers. "Maybe not so much here. But most other places. People will really need our help."

"Very true." Ms. Martin nodded. "How is your coat drive coming?"

Sylvie had noticed the collection box in the hall was at least half full by now. It was a beginning, but she needed more coats. Many, many more! Luckily, Sylvie had the perfect plan to get them.

"It's coming!" she replied.

Sylvie grabbed rainbow glitter from the imagination station. It would add a stellar accent to her talent show costumes and help one of her acts win.

She could picture the glittery getups now. Even better, she could picture the coat drive announcement in the newspaper after one of her acts won.

She thought of all the buzz it would create. All the coats they would collect. All the people they would help.

But, at the bulletin board, Sylvie's eyes fixed on the most unperfect and un-stellar thing of all.

DRESS REHEARSAL

Standing in the school office with the phone to her ear, Sylvie pictured the sign on the bulletin board. "Talent Show Rehearsal After School," it had read.

Sylvie shifted the receiver to her other ear. "Yep, it's today," she said to her dad. "And every day this week. So I'll be staying late."

"Sounds exciting," her dad said. "Break a leg!"

She really wished he hadn't said that. Thinking about the gymnastics moves and song arrangements she had to learn, Sylvie's stomach started to do some flips of its own.

Sylvie went to the bathroom and slipped into her star-covered leotard. She pulled on her sweatbands and affixed her glitter bandages. They looked much better than the plain old brown Band-Aids Camilla used to wear.

Her stomach was feeling nervous. Sylvie couldn't help but admire the outfit she had put together for her and Camilla's gymnastics act.

"Achoo!" A sneeze echoed through the bathroom. "Achoo! Achoo! Achoo!"

Sylvie looked down. Two puffball socks peeked out of the stall next to her. "Camilla?"

"Hey," said Camilla. "Achoo! Ready for dress rehearsal? I'm so excited. I've been practicing extra hard on my double backflips."

Sylvie hadn't had time to practice her gymnastics moves. She had been so focused on organizing things for the coat drive and the talent show. She felt butterflies in her stomach and looked up at the ceiling.

"Dress rehearsal, sure. Double backflips? Can't wait."

Suddenly, the bathroom echoed with the sound of a group of sea lions. Huh? Was that Camilla coughing?

"Excuse me," said Camilla. "Do you have any tissues? I'm all out."

Sylvie passed a tissue under the stall.

"I heard about that snowstorm that went out to sea. I can't believe how cold it gets in other parts of the country,"

Camilla said. "I'll bring in a coat to donate tomorrow."

Sylvie's eyes brightened. "Thanks."

It was great to hear Camilla excited about the coat drive. Now Sylvie needed to put aside her organizing and practice her performances.

"See you there."

Sylvie ducked out of the bathroom and raced down the hall.

Sylvie had the cafeteria-gymnasium to herself. She would start by warming up with some old Tumble Tuesdays magic.

Sylvie crouched on the stacked blue mat and pushed off. She wound up on her stomach, under the salad bar.

"What in the world?" Sylvie cried, pushing a bowl of coleslaw off of her

head. "Nope! A little shredded cabbage is not going to stop me!"

She got up and tried again. And again. But none of her gymnastics moves clicked. She tried some more.

The doors swung open. More third graders rushed inside for dress rehearsal.

Sylvie kept trying. She tried over and over until the cafeteria-gymnasium was packed with other performers. There was no space left to tumble.

"Uh-oh," she whispered, letting out a deep sigh. She must not have been a gymnast extraordinaire after all.

Camilla walked over. She reached out and helped Sylvie up. "Thanks," Sylvie said, slumping against the wall. "But I guess I can't be in your act after all."

Camilla opened her mouth to respond, but all that came out were sneezes.

Josh, Nick, and Malik huddled and sang while they waited for the rehearsal to begin. She walked slowly over to them. A sinking feeling washed over her. They sounded great. Really great. *Uh-oh*, she thought.

"Ready for your solo?" asked Josh.

"Did you memorize the lyrics?" asked Nick.

"Can you hit those high notes?" asked Malik.

Sylvie picked shredded carrot out of her hair and tried to come up with something to say. No, she hadn't memorized the lyrics. Or been able to hit the high notes.

Sylvie felt her face warm. Her friends had spent weeks learning the lyrics and training their voices.

She had to be realistic. The few days remaining wouldn't be enough time to learn the acts. Even for Sylvie.

Sylvie blinked back tears. She wasn't a gymnast extraordinaire. She wasn't a singer extraordinaire.

She might not have any talent at all, she realized. She would never win the talent show or be featured in the *Sea View Times*. What would come of the coat drive now?

GONE VIRAL

The rest of the week at Sea View Elementary had flown by in a whirlwind of glitter bandages, chopped karate boards, and half-eaten hot dogs.

Minutes before the talent show, Sylvie popped into the bathroom. "Ouch!" She felt some stiffness across her sore shoulders.

Sylvie set down her binder and stretched her arms high. "OK, back. Be strong," Sylvie told her reflection. There was no time for back trouble! She had enough trouble already.

Sylvie had had to face facts. She couldn't tumble. She couldn't sing. It turned out she wouldn't be performing in the talent show. Even worse, she might not have anything extraordinary about her.

Ms. Thompson told Sylvie she could still help her with organizing the show to make sure things ran smoothly. Sylvie agreed; she was never one to let a teacher down.

But she was heartbroken. There was no way the coat drive would be mentioned in the *Sea View Times* now.

Ms. Martin walked in and straightened her rhinestoned panda brooch in the mirror. She leaned over and glanced at the map on the cover of Sylvie's binder. Then she pointed to the coat donation boxes. "That's a lot of donation boxes," said Ms. Martin.

"We have over fifty now!" Sylvie said, perking up. It *was* a big amount. "Everyone has one: the library, Sea View Laser Tag, the food truck outside city hall. Even Tents & Tents. And those are just a few."

Sylvie realized why her back was sore! She'd carried a lot of boxes. And collected a lot of coats too. Her heart started to feel a little less broken.

"Terrific work," said Ms. Martin. "And I noticed you created lots of buzz around town. Looks like all the signs, calls, texts, emails, social media, and door-to-door outreach worked."

"Yeah, it's pretty stellar," said Sylvie, excited. "I've made four trips to collect coats from the lifeguard stand alone!

And everyone in the talent show has helped, too."

"Amazing!" Ms. Martin said as she pulled open the bathroom door. "See you soon."

Sylvie peeked at the coat drive map on her binder once more. Soon her heart felt even better.

The emails and social media posts she and her friends had written started in the neighborhood group. Then people forwarded them to friends. Soon they took off further than anyone could have imagined!

Unfortunately, the coat drive wasn't the only thing that had gone viral.

Camilla's sneezy fall cold had gone viral too. By Friday, nearly half the school seemed to be stuck home with the cold, or caught in sneezing fits in their classrooms.

Sylvie did one last stretch and then staked her position as program distributor at the cafeteria gymnasium doors. She handed her neighbor, Mr. Wolf, a program.

"Welcome to Sea View Elementary's talent show. Please note, Ms. Bachrach is out sick. Her performance of "I Am Woman" will be played by Coach Ken."

Sammy rushed over. "Sylvie! I'm so sorry," he said.

"Huh?" Sylvie asked, looking down at some notes.

"I was helping feed Brownie and Ham-Ham in the media center," he said. "I overheard Ms. Thompson just went home with a fever."

Sylvie looked up. "A fever? No! Poor Ms. Thompson."

"Yeah. I ran out when I learned the news," said Sammy. "I didn't even give the hamsters their dessert! I knew you'd want to know right away."

"Thanks Sammy. I'll be sure to make a get-well card for Ms. Thompson after the talent show."

Sammy gulped. "Sylvie, there's more."

"More?"

"Unfortunately, yes," he continued. "Principal Close said unless someone else can run the talent show, it will need to be postponed. Maybe until spring. She's about to make an announcement to the audience."

"Postponed?! Until spring?" She threw her hands up. "It can't be!"

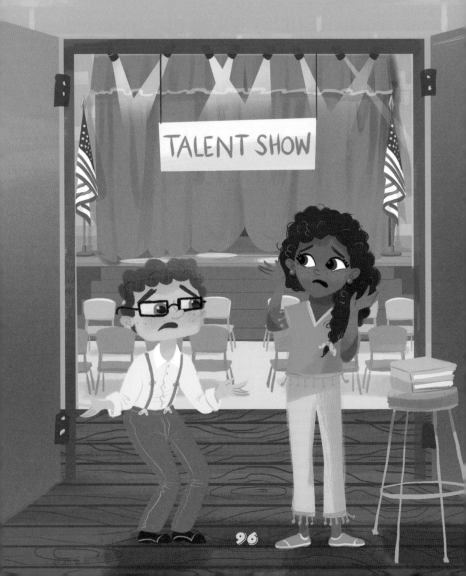

ORGANIZER EXTRAORDINAIRE

The show couldn't be postponed! Sylvie had to get through to Principal Close before she made the announcement.

She shoved her things into Sammy's arms. She dashed backstage and rifled through a crate marked "tech gear."

"Gotcha!" she said, pulling out a headset. The headset was what Ms. Thompson used to communicate with Principal Close, teachers, and parent volunteers during the show. Now Sylvie could get a message to them!

"Sylvie?" someone hollered from the audience. She peeked out from behind the curtain. Her things were about to fall out of Sammy's arms and topple all over the first row. Sammy needed help.

Sylvie waved. "Over here!"

Sammy came backstage.

Sylvie adjusted Ms. Thompson's

headset and clipped it on. She carefully slid her megaphone and programs out from Sammy's arms.

She pointed to the binder he was holding and covered her mouthpiece. "Tab two," she said. "The pre-show checklist." Sammy understood. He frantically turned the pages.

Sylvie cleared her throat. She pressed down on the talk button. "Principal Close, Ms. Martin, teachers, and parent volunteers."

Static screeched in Sylvie's ear. The headset wasn't working!

Sylvie shook her head. She tried again. "Principal Close, Ms. Martin, teachers, and parent volunteers."

Nothing.

Guests continued filing in. Parents, grandparents, friends, and neighbors too. Flower bouquets and coat donations were piled in their arms.

Sylvie's family was seated in the front row. Her heart raced. There was no postponing now. She had to get to Principal Close!

She jiggled the headset. "C'mon!" She noticed the channel setting and turned the dial. "Principal Close, Ms. Martin, teachers, and parent volunteers."

Voices floated in through her ear. Finally!

"Unfortunately Ms. Thompson went home with a fever," Principal Close was saying. "With so many teachers out sick, and because many of us were out sick earlier in the week, we have no one to organize tonight's talent show. We'll need to postpone—"

"Wait!" Sylvie interrupted.

Nothing.

"Hold on!" Sylvie yelled.

At last, her voice piped through the headsets. Even if it came through sounding kind of funny.

"Ms. Thompson?" Principal Close sounded confused. "I thought you went home. We were just going to postpone. We have no one else who could organize like you can."

"Not Ms. Thompson. It's Sylvie."

Sylvie thought about the stellar organizing she had done for her friends' acts. She thought about how she'd helped Ms. Thompson all week. She knew she could do this!

Sylvie scanned her checklist over Sammy's shoulder. *Stellar organizing,* she thought. Then a realization hit her like a trillion gallons of water pounding her favorite Amazon rain forest.

Maybe she couldn't participate in the talent show for gymnastics, singing, or skydiving. But she, Sylvie Schwartz, was not without a talent. Organizing was her talent!

"Sylvie?" asked Principal Close. "Are you offering to direct the talent show?"

The seats had filled up. It was getting harder to hear.

Sylvie raised her voice. "Yes! I know I can do it!"

Ms. Martin's voice came through next. "Sylvie, do you know all the cues and details? Can you keep things organized and run the show tonight?"

Sylvie looked at the program. She saw her teacher across the room.

"You've got this," mouthed Ms. Martin, covering her microphone with one hand. She gave Sylvie a thumbs-up with the other.

A smile spread across Sylvie's face. She tightened the headset and pressed the talk button. "Yes, Ms. Martin. Sylvie Schwartz, Organizer Extraordinaire at your service!"

"Well, OK, then," Principal Close said.

Sylvie breathed a sigh of relief. "Let's do this," she said to Sammy. Sylvie pulled out her megaphone and raced to the room where kids and teachers were supposed to be getting ready.

The pre-show energy and excitement was supposed to be electric. But the performers were not warming up their high notes. They were speaking in low whispers. Heads hung. Shoulders slumped. Sylvie realized that they hadn't heard the good news yet.

"People, we've had a slight change of plans," Sylvie said. "Ms. Thompson can't be here, but the show must go on. We've got all these acts. All these people in the audience."

The smell of hot dogs wafted through the air. She giggled. "And these cooked hot dogs."

Someone opened a window, and a cool breeze blew into the room. *The cold was coming*, Sylvie thought.

"And, whoever wins, can you please mention the coat drive in the paper? We have over fifty drop-off locations across town."

Zaki tucked a napkin over his T-shirt. "I'm in," he said. "I will!"

Josh pointed his thumbs at his chest. "Me too!"

Tori and Lori got on their toes. They nodded. "And us!"

Camilla burst into the room. She tossed her tissue box into a corner and dipped her hands in chalk. "Ready when you are."

"Five minutes," Principal Close announced over the headsets.

Sylvie huddled with some crew helpers by the lighting rig. Carefully, they reviewed every item on her list. The alarm on Sylvie's watch beeped.

"Showtime!" she cheered. Sylvie cued the lights. She signaled the sound. She slipped Camilla a glittery Band-Aid.

Spotlights washed the cafeteria auditorium stage. Music rang from the speakers. The curtains opened.

Sylvie marked a check next to the last item in the pre-show checklist. She flipped the page.

The next sixty minutes flew by in a well-organized blur of the most extraordinary gymnastics, singing, karate chopping, and hot dog eating Sea View Elementary had to offer.

SEA VIEW TIMES
SEA VIEW ORGANIZER
EXTRAORDINAIRE

Sea View Elementary third grader Sylvie Schwartz and her organizational talents saved the day when a cold threatened to take down the entire school talent show.

With nearly half of teachers and students out sick during the week, Ms. Schwartz gave her all, and then some, to keep the show on track. Self-proclaimed "organizer extraordinaire," Ms. Schwartz commented, "Everyone has different talents. Mine happens to be organizing."

When asked for examples of other things she's organized, Ms. Schwartz answered, "I'm so glad you brought that up! Most recently, I've organized Sea View's largest coat drive in history. It has been extended through the weekend to allow *Sea View Times* readers a chance to donate. New and gently used coats and jackets can be dropped off at any of the more than fifty locations across Sea View. Spread the word!"

RELATED:
Pianist Extraordinaire Omeed Khan Wins Sea View Elementary Talent Show Performing Mr. Twist 'N' Shout Classic: 'The Sunblock Rock'

HOW TO HOLD A COAT DRIVE:

1. Plan your drive

2. Register your drive

3. Promote your drive (create lots of buzz!)

4. Start your drive

5. Celebrate your drive

6. Deliver your coats

For more information, please visit:

https://www.onewarmcoat.org/holdacoatdrive/